DRAGONBREATH
ATTACK OF THE NINJA FROGS

*This one's for Mom, who believed in me
even when there was no supporting evidence*

DIAL BOOKS
An imprint of Penguin Group (USA) Inc.
Published by The Penguin Group • Penguin Group (USA) Inc., 375 Hudson Street, New York, NY
10014, U.S.A. • Penguin Group (Canada), 90 Eglinton Avenue East, Suite 700, Toronto, Ontario,
Canada M4P 2Y3 (a division of Pearson Penguin Canada Inc.) • Penguin Books Ltd, 80 Strand,
London WC2R 0RL, England • Penguin Ireland, 25 St. Stephen's Green, Dublin 2, Ireland (a
division of Penguin Books Ltd) • Penguin Group (Australia), 250 Camberwell Road, Camberwell,
Victoria 3124, Australia (a division of Pearson Australia Group Pty Ltd) • Penguin Books India
Pvt Ltd, 11 Community Centre, Panchsheel Park, New Delhi - 110 017, India • Penguin Group
(NZ), 67 Apollo Drive, Rosedale, North Shore 0632, New Zealand (a division of Pearson
New Zealand Ltd) • Penguin Books (South Africa) (Pty) Ltd, 24 Sturdee Avenue, Rosebank,
Johannesburg 2196, South Africa •Penguin Books Ltd, Registered Offices: 80 Strand, London
WC2R 0RL, England

The publisher does not have any control over and does not assume
any responsibility for author or third-party websites or their content.
Text set in Stempel Schneidler
Printed in the U.S.A.
10 9 8

Library of Congress Cataloging-in-Publication Data

Vernon, Ursula.
    Dragonbreath: attack of the ninja frogs / by Ursula Vernon.
        p. cm.
    Summary: When Suki the salamander—the new foreign exchange student—is being stalked
by ninja frogs, Danny, Wendell the iguana, and Suki travel to Great-Grandfather Dragonbreath's
home in mythical Japan to find a solution to the problem.
    ISBN 978-0-8037-3365-7 (hardcover)
    [1. Ninja—Fiction. 2. Dragons—Fiction. 3. Reptiles—Fiction. 4. Amphibians—Fiction.
5. Friendship—Fiction. 6. Japan—Fiction] I. Title.
    PZ7.V5985Drd 2010
    [Fic]—dc22
                                2009012273

DRAGONBREATH
ATTACK OF THE NINJA FROGS

BY
URSULA VERNON

DIAL BOOKS

an imprint of Penguin Group (USA) Inc.

FEUDAL JAPAN. LORD DRAGONBREATH, RULER OF AN ANCIENT SAMURAI CLAN, ADDRESSES HIS TROOPS ON THE EVE OF BATTLE.
LORD DRAGONBREATH!

KUNG FU DREAMS

Danny Dragonbreath tried to remember what he had been thinking about, and couldn't. Something about samurai, and cliff tops, and snapping banners, like in *Swords of Izumo,* which had been on last night. He tried to sink back into his daydream, but it was long gone.

Danny sighed. Pepperoni pizza was a good thing—possibly even a *great* thing—but not as awesome as kung fu movies. Hardly anything was.

Still, he couldn't be too upset. *Seven Fists of Carnage* was going to be on tonight. He hoped it was as good as his all-time favorite, *Vengeance of the Thirteen Masters,* in which a blind salamander samurai fights off thirteen ninja clans, using only a pair of chopsticks.

Danny passed the time until the pizza arrived by drawing ninjas. Drawing ninjas was difficult because you couldn't really see a ninja. So the drawings mostly consisted of places where ninjas might be hiding.

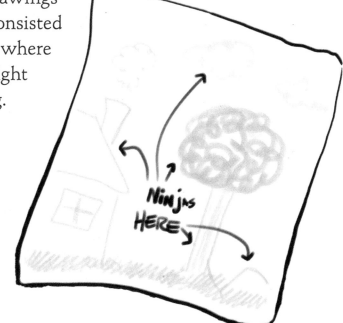

"Danny! Pizza!"

Danny hurried down the stairs. Halfway down, he paused to do a kung fu move from *Thirteen Masters,* nearly tripped over his own tail, and went down the rest of the stairs a bit faster than he'd planned.

"Furious Crane Falls From Above!"

Mr. Dragonbreath paused, pizza boxes in hand. "Is that what kids are calling pizza these days?"

Danny slid into his chair. "No, Dad. I was just practicing my kung fu moves."

Mr. Dragonbreath chose to let this pass. Danny loaded his plate with pizza.

"Mom, Dad, can I eat in the living room? *Seven Fists of Carnage* is going to be on!"

"I'm not sure if all these violent movies are good for you . . ." Mr. Dragonbreath said.

"Daaaaaaad! C'mon!"

"A compelling argument," said Danny's mom. "But no eating in the living room. You always get tomato sauce on the rug."

Danny began wolfing the slices down as quickly as possible.

"Try to breathe between bites," said his father dryly.

"Mmmmghff!"

Danny washed his third slice down with soda, and stifled a belch. "Thankyouthatwasgreatmay-Ibeexcused?" he rattled off.

"What's so great about *Six Fangs of Cabbage*?" asked his father.

"*Seven Fists of Carnage!*" Danny waved his hands in the air. "Sheesh, Dad! Now can I pleeeeease be excused?"

"Yes, yes, go on . . ." Mr. Dragonbreath waved him off. Danny sprinted for the living room.

"Three slices in twenty-six seconds," said his mother. "New record."

"He takes after your side of the family, you know," said Danny's father mournfully, and helped himself to another slice of pizza.

NERDS IN LOVE

Danny jogged toward the bus stop. If he missed the bus, he'd have to go back and get his father to drive him to school. And *then* he would have to listen to ten minutes of why he could breathe fire if he just applied himself.

Besides, he'd hate to miss Wendell. Danny had to know what his best friend thought of *Seven Fists of Carnage*. There was this one bit where the gecko hero had fought off the hordes of chameleon ninjas, while sticking upside down to the ceiling and holding a dagger in his tongue.

Danny rounded the corner and realized abruptly that Wendell had other things on his mind.

Wendell was talking to a *girl.*

Not just enforced in-class talking either—not "Can I borrow your notes?" or "Do you know the answer to number #17?" *Actual* talking, like you would with your friends.

It was unprecedented!

It was madness!

It was just begging for cooties!

As the dragon watched, mildly aghast, Wendell pulled a book out of his backpack and handed it to the girl in question.

Danny approached slowly. Now that he was closer, he recognized the girl as Suki the salamander, an exchange student from somewhere or other in Japan.

Well, she was smart, like Wendell. Maybe they were talking about . . . whatever nerds talked about . . . science or standardized tests or something.

"*The Stone of Tears!*" he then heard Suki say. "Thank you so much, Wendell!" Suki hugged the book to her chest. "I'll get it back to you soon."

"Oh . . . well . . . I . . . uh . . . take your time . . ." Wendell was having trou-

ble making eye contact suddenly, and his words seemed to have dried up. "I mean . . . there's no . . . Oh, hey, Danny."

"Hey, Wendell," said Danny. "Hey . . . um . . . Suki."

"Hi, Danny." She bobbed her head.

An awkward silence fell.

Danny, who had previously thought that talking to a girl was bad, rapidly discovered that *not* talking to a girl was much worse. What did girls talk about? Ponies or unicorns or . . .

"So, um . . . do you like . . . err . . . unicorns?" Danny felt like he was wading through molasses.

Suki stared at him, tilting her head to one side as if he were an interesting bug. "I've never met one," she said finally. "Given that they're imaginary and all."

"Oh." Danny *had* met one once—she'd come to his second cousin's wedding and had a trained helper monkey that fed her canapés.

But this seemed like a lot of work to explain.

"Er," Danny said instead. "Cool."

Wendell seemed to have shut down completely. Danny elbowed him to make sure he hadn't died standing up.

Wendell grunted. "Um. It's . . . um . . . nice weather we're having. . . ."

Danny and Suki looked up. It was gray and rather overcast. Wendell hunched his shoulders, looking more like a turtle than an iguana.

Fortunately, before anybody was forced to make any more conversation, the bus pulled up.

It occurred to Danny, quite horribly, that Suki might want to sit with Wendell on the bus. And if Wendell and Suki sat together, then Danny would have to sit somewhere else. Alone.

No, no. That was crazy. His best friend would never abandon him for a *girl*.

Fortunately, Wendell showed

no sign of wanting to sit anywhere other than their usual seats, and Suki was already sprawled out in her own seat, deep into a book.

Danny and Wendell sat down. Wendell appeared very interested in something on the other side of the window, possibly waiting for the "nice weather" to arrive. Danny wasn't letting go that easily.

"So, is that your *girlfriend*?"

"No!" Wendell glared at him, shoving his glasses up higher on his nose. "I was just loaning her a comic book."

"A comic book?" Danny rolled his eyes. "I didn't know you read girl comics. What was it, *Lizard Sparkle Princess* or something?"

"It was *Empire of Feathers*," said Wendell with dignity.

Danny paused. He had to admit, *Empire of Feathers* was actually quite respectable reading. It was about an alternate universe where birds ruled the world. It was dark and gritty and had lots of battle scenes and intrigue and poisonings and magic, and a clan of rooster assassins that wore cloaks made of their victim's feathers.

"She reads *Empire of Feathers*?"

"It never came out in Japan, so she couldn't get it over there, and she really wanted to read it. You would have done the same thing."

"She reads *Arm of the Yakuza* too, and she wants to be a veterinarian," Wendell added proudly.

"Don't most of the girls in our class want to be veterinarians?" asked Danny. "At Career Day there were like ten veterinarians, two nurses, and Christiana Vanderpool wanted to be a brain surgeon. What is it with girls and medical professions?"

"Well . . . maybe . . ." Wendell vividly remembered Christiana's presentation, which had involved a sheep's brain she'd brought from home. "But Suki really could. She's totally smart."

"Yeah, yeah," muttered Danny, kicking the seat in front of him. "Nerds in love. I get it."

Danny grinned. "Uh-huh. You're doomed."

Wendell lifted his snout and pointedly ignored his friend until the bus pulled up to the front of the school.

They were climbing up the steps when Wendell asked, very quietly, "Do you think she'd *like* chocolates?"

Danny sighed. "Completely doomed."

A LONG DAY

The first half of the school day passed in the usual fashion—slowly and with homework. Danny slouched down in his seat and stared at the clock.

In the back of the classroom, Big Eddy the Komodo dragon was eating an eraser. (He did this at least once a week, forgetting it wasn't bubble gum.)

Danny looked out the window.

If ninjas were going to come in—and why ninjas would want to invade Mr. Snaug's science class was anybody's guess, unless ninjas had some kind of aversion to geology—they'd probably slide down from the roof on ropes. Then they'd smash through the windows, glass raining everywhere. Big Eddy would try to hit one, and they'd knock him down with one of those amazing one-fingered finishing moves. Then Danny would have to stand up, surrounded by broken glass and scattered homework, and he would show them Drunken Crane Style and all the ninjas would pull back, realizing that they were facing a true kung fu master and—

"Mister Dragonbreath," said Mr. Snaug. Danny jerked guiltily back to reality.

"Um . . ."

"Do you know the answer to the question?" Mr. Snaug was a long-tailed gecko, and sometimes if he caught you not paying attention, he'd smack his tail down on the desk in front of you and make you jump a foot in the air.

"Uhhhh. . . ." Danny looked frantically at Wendell. Wendell put his head in his hands, an indication that the answer was too complicated to try and express in mime. What had Mr. Snaug been talking about? Plate tectonics—something about continents or rocks or something—

"Hot lava?" he tried hopefully.

Mr. Snaug rubbed a hand over his face, looking rather like Wendell for a moment. "Danny, are you telling me that the theory of continental drift was first proposed by . . . hot lava?"

The other students giggled. Danny flushed bronze and slid farther down in his chair.

"Anyone?" Mr. Snaug looked around the room.

Wendell put his hand up. Mr. Snaug rolled his eyes. "I know YOU know, Wendell. Anyone else? Suki?"

"The theory of continental drift was proposed by Alfred Wegener," said Suki, and cast an apologetic glance over at Danny.

Wendell put his hand down and gazed admiringly at Suki. Danny's mild embarrassment was replaced with mild nausea.

"Very good," said Mr. Snaug. "Now, class, if you'll open to page seventy-nine, you'll

see that Wegener's theory was not met with immediate acceptance . . ."

The room filled with the rustle of paper. Danny grabbed for his fleeting daydream of being a kung fu master, but all he could think of was hot lava. He sighed.

Oh well. It wasn't realistic anyway. Ninjas were sneaky. They probably wouldn't smash through the window. They'd climb into the vents and blow poisoned black lotus pollen down into the classroom, and Mr. Snaug would fall asleep and—

"Mister Dragonbreath, are you paying attention?"

"Yes, Mr. Snaug," said Danny glumly, and resigned himself to the grip of education.

THE BATHROOM WALL

"Plate tectonics," said Danny bitterly as he left the lunch line with a tray full of corn dogs. "When are we ever going to use THAT?"

Wendell met him, holding his sack lunch. "Well, if you ever wanted to be a scientist . . . or a science teacher . . ." He trailed off. Wendell had a pretty good imagination, but there were limits.

"I'm going to be a kung fu master," said Danny.

"Subduction Zone Strikes From Below!" said Wendell, and snickered.

Danny waited for this example of nerd humor to pass. "Where should we sit?"

They surveyed the cafeteria.

"There's some open seats over there—"

"Big Eddy," said Danny, jerking his head in that direction. Wendell grimaced.

Big Eddy the Komodo dragon was the class bully. He was huge. He wore T-shirts bigger than Mr. Snaug's, and he had never forgiven Danny for an incident with some very angry potato salad earlier in the year.

"I think there's an open table over there," said Wendell, pointing in the other direction.

"I wish we didn't always have to worry about Big Eddy," Danny grumbled. Hiding from the school bully was not terribly kung-fu-master-worthy behavior.

"Well, he *is* your nemesis."

"He is?" Danny had only seen the word in comic books before. Trust Wendell to use it in actual conversation.

"Sure."

"Neat!"

"She's an exchange student, she doesn't know most of the other girls," Wendell said.

"But she's a girl!"

"So?"

Danny grabbed his friend's shoulder. Wendell seemed to be missing the key point. "Wendell, listen to me! She's a *girl*!"

"Fine," hissed Wendell. "Name one good reason we shouldn't eat with a girl!"

Danny paused, mouth open. "Cooties."

"Cooties," said Wendell grimly. He shoved his glasses up his snout. "Listen carefully to me. There is *no such thing* as cooties. What are you, *five*?"

Danny took a large bite of corn dog to give himself time to think. No such thing as cooties? Wendell was pretty good about knowing what existed, but then again, he was obviously dangerously insane at the moment, and it was up to Danny to provide the voice of reason.*

"There are totally cooties," he said.

"There are not."

* Across the city, emergency crews, school nurses, and Danny's parents got a sudden cold chill down their spines.

"They're not real. They're imaginary. They're a myth."

"A myth!" Danny gestured with his corn dog, nearly taking Wendell's nose off. "Like dragons are a myth?"

"Uh—"

LIKE SEA SERPENTS AND GIANT SQUID ARE MYTHS, OR DID YOU FORGET OUR LITTLE TRIP LAST MONTH?

Wendell shuddered. He still had occasional nightmares about the crushing tentacles of the giant squid from his underwater trip with Danny.

Before he could marshal any more arguments, Suki came through one of the doors. She was walking very fast with her head down.

Unfortunately she walked right into Big Eddy.

"Uh-oh," said Wendell.

Without quite knowing how it happened, Wendell found himself jumping to his feet. Vague notions of hero-ism entered his mind, and then paused, confused by their sur-roundings.

The Komodo dragon, never quick to react, blinked down at the little salamander. She barely came up to his stomach. Suki stared up the length of Big Eddy's pizza-stained T-shirt at him.

"Sorry," she mumbled, turn-ing away.

Big Eddy's forehead fur-rowed into a frown. "Did you just run into me, squirt?"

Wendell began trying to make his way down the aisle.

Danny, realizing that Wendell was about to do something profoundly stupid, hurried after him. (He wasn't quite clear on whether he was going to stop Wendell doing something stupid, or help him do something stupid, but after all, that's what friends are for.)

"Wendell!" he hissed, catching up with the iguana. "Don't be an idiot! Big Eddy won't hit a girl!"

"Does Big Eddy know that?" Wendell hissed back.

"Sorry," said Suki again, trying to move away. Eddy's cronies, Harry the chameleon and Jason, a salamander rather larger and uglier than Suki, blocked her path.

"You oughta watch where you're going, squirt," said Eddy.

"It was an accident," said Suki, sounding ready to cry.

Wendell skidded past the last table and raised a trembling fist.

Danny had a vision of Wendell being pounded into the ground like a tent peg. Big Eddy's fists were bigger than the iguana's head.

Wendell drew a deep breath and opened his mouth. "Y-you leave her—"

Big Eddy turned.

"Hey, Big Eddy!" said Danny, jumping in front of his friend. "Did you know somebody wrote something rude about you in the second-floor bathroom?"

Eddy blinked at him. "What was that, dork-breath?"

"In the third stall. I'm just telling you."

Big Eddy shook his head, like a horse shaking off flies. It was difficult for him to change thoughts that quickly. "Somebody wrote somethin' about me?"

Danny nodded, eyes wide and innocent. "You might want to go scribble it out. I don't think I'd want anybody saying that about *my* mother."

Big Eddy growled and turned away, Suki forgotten. His flunkies fell in hastily behind him as the

Komodo dragon went in search of the graffiti.

On the way out of the cafeteria, he reached out and grabbed Danny's lunch. Danny watched his corn dog exit with the rest of Big Eddy's entourage and sighed.

"You okay?" asked Wendell.

"Yeah, I'm fine." Suki wrapped her arms around herself. "Just should have looked where I was going . . ."

"Come and eat lunch with us," said Wendell.

Danny stifled another sigh. On the one hand, cooties—on the other hand, his parents always said that you came together and helped each other in times of crisis. He was pretty sure they'd meant earthquakes and tornados and lance-wielding knights, but Big Eddy was a natural disaster all on his own.

They sat down. Suki sat across from them. Danny wasn't sure how much eye contact you were supposed to make with girls—did you look at them, or didn't you look at them? If you looked at them, were you staring?

Suki solved the problem by mostly staring at her lunch. So did Wendell. Danny stared at the ceiling and wondered when the situation had gotten out of control.

"Thank you for chasing off Big Eddy," said Suki after a long pause. She picked at her sandwich. "Is there really something written on the bathroom wall?"

"There sure is," said Danny proudly. It had taken him twenty minutes with a protractor, and he'd needed Wendell's help spelling some of the bigger words.

"That was very nice of you," said Suki.

"Well, he *is* my nemesis," said Danny.

Wendell rolled his eyes.

WEBBED WARRIORS

It had been a long lunch and an even longer day at school. Danny was glad to finally be away from Big Eddy, plate tectonics, and Suki.

Unfortunately, fate did not seem to be on Danny's side today. He and Wendell were walking home along the edge of Birchbark Park when they heard a scream. Both of them froze.

"What do we *dooo*?" asked Wendell, paling.

It was an interesting question. If somebody was being murdered, you were supposed to get the police, but at the same time, if you could stay and be a world-famous hero—well, you'd hate to *miss* it.

"I think we're supposed to get a teacher or policeman or something—" said Danny's mouth, while the rest of Danny was busy shoving through the hedge and into the park.

"This doesn't look like getting a policeman," said Wendell.

"Maybe we'll run into one on the way."

Danny's tail vanished through the hedge. Wendell realized that he was alone with a murderer on the loose and hurriedly shoved through the hedge after him.

There was another scream. This one sounded more mad, and it seemed to be coming from behind the little building with the restrooms.

"GO AWAY!"

"I think it's Suki!" said Wendell. He gritted his teeth, lowered his head, and suddenly Danny was running to try and keep up with his best friend.

"Wendell, wait!" Danny was confident of his ability to handle a murderer—he almost knew kung fu, after all, and he'd even breathed fire once under extreme duress—but he wasn't so confident of Wendell's skills. If Wendell was in a kung fu movie, he would be listed in the credits as "Screaming Victim #4."

"She's in trouble!"

"LEAVE ME ALONE!"

Somebody was in trouble . . . but judging by the tone of voice, Danny thought it might be Suki's attacker. The dragon put on an extra burst of speed, and he and Wendell skidded around the corner of the building together.

Suki was hanging between two creatures, kicking at them and slapping furiously with her tail.

Danny knew that they had to go rescue her—that was just what you *did*—but for a moment, all he could do was stare.

Suki's attackers were identical. They wore black suits that covered everything but their eyes, and they had broad, sticky pads on their fingers. One of them had a pair of sais* shoved into his belt.

They were frogs.

Ninja frogs.

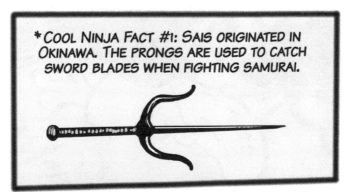

*COOL NINJA FACT #1: SAIS ORIGINATED IN OKINAWA. THE PRONGS ARE USED TO CATCH SWORD BLADES WHEN FIGHTING SAMURAI.

"Holy mackerel," breathed Danny. "Ninjas!"

The frogs stared at Danny and Wendell. Danny and Wendell stared at the frogs. Suki wrenched herself sideways and cracked her tail across one's foot.

It occurred to Danny that he ought to do something, but they were *real live ninjas* and—and—

His thoughts pretty much stopped after that.

The two ninja frogs looked at each other, then, as one, dropped Suki and leaped onto the roof.

They cleared it in a single bound, went over the top, and were gone from sight.

"Oh my God," said Danny. "Oh my God—oh— did you see— ninja *frogs—* thatisthecool- estthing*ever*!"

Wendell and Suki stared at him as if he'd lost his mind.

"Are you okay?" Wendell asked Suki.

"—real live ninjas and they had masks and sais —ohmyGodohmyGodohmyGodohmyGodoh-myGod—"

Suki stood up and brushed herself off. "I'm fine, I guess."

"Are they still around? Should we get out of here?"

"—I wonder if they know ninjitsu they must 'cause they're ninjas I wonder if they could teach me—"

"They're probably still around," said Suki gloomily, "but they only seem to come after me when nobody else is here. Thanks for showing up."

"What did they want?" Wendell wanted to know.

"I wish I knew. They just started—Danny, will you *shut up* already?"

Suki sat down on a park bench. "I think they're coming after me. I started seeing things—just out of the corner of my eye—but there was one outside my window this morning, and then one nearly jumped me outside the girls' bathroom."

Danny took his hands off his mouth and managed to say, in a normal tone of voice, "Well, at least they waited until you were outside the bathroom."

"Maybe they don't have any girl ninjas to send in, I don't know." Suki folded her arms.

"But why are they coming after you?"

"I don't know!" Suki threw her hands in the air. "They didn't say anything! They just grabbed me and tried to haul me somewhere! I don't know what's going on!"

"Have you told somebody? Maybe your host parents?" asked Wendell.

"Oh, yeah, that'd work really well," said Suki bitterly. "'Mr. and Mrs. Schwartz, please don't think I'm crazy, but I'm being attacked by ninjas.'

The *best* thing that could happen is that they'd tell me I had an overactive imagination from reading too many comic books."

"That's true," said Danny, who had listened to that particular speech at least three times himself.*

"I guess I'll find out what they want when they finally manage to kidnap me," said Suki, kicking the park bench savagely.

"We won't let that happen!" said Wendell. "Will we, Danny?"

"Hmm? What?" Danny had fallen off the side of the bench and was on his hands and knees on the ground.

"Danny!"

"Sorry." Danny held up a bit of metal. "I think one of them dropped this."

"What's that spiral design?" Suki wanted to know.

* Danny felt that this was completely unfair. His overactive imagination had a number of sources, only one of which was comic books.

> *COOL NINJA FACT #2: THE WORD "SHURIKEN" MEANS "SWORD HIDDEN IN THE HAND." IT'S A TRADITIONAL NINJA THROWING WEAPON THAT COMES IN A VARIETY OF SHAPES.

"Some kind of sigil," Wendell said.

"The what now?" said Danny.

"Their sign. A picture like a signature."

"Maybe it's the sign of the ninja clan." Danny propped his snout up on his hand. "Maybe they followed you from Japan. Maybe your father's in the Yakuza, like in *Painted Shadows*, and they're trying to get at him by kidnapping you—"

"My father's a botanist," interrupted Suki. "He studies corn."

Danny was never one to let a promising idea go.

All three of them sat in silence for a minute. Wendell scanned the trees nervously for shadowy amphibian figures.

"We can't just let ninjas get you," he said.

Suki smiled faintly. "Thanks."

"Well," said Danny, leaning back, "ninjas are Japanese, so what do you do back home in Japan when you get a case of ninjas?"

WE DON'T! THERE AREN'T ANY NINJAS! REAL PEOPLE DON'T GET NINJAS!

Danny put his hands up defensively. "Jeez, no need to yell—"

"You're an idiot!" Suki yelled.

This did not faze Danny, who had been called much worse things, occasionally by the emergency room staff. (Seriously, though, why would anyone make chocolate-flavored laxatives? It was just *asking* for trouble.) "I was just saying—"

"Japan isn't some kind of fantasy land full of ninjas!" Suki said. "I mean, they're practically mythological!"

Danny snapped his fingers. "That's it!"

"Oh no." Wendell put his hands over his eyes.

"What?" Suki looked confused.

Danny jumped to his feet. "C'mon! Let's go to my house!"

"Whaaaat...?"

"I know all about mythology," said Danny as Wendell and Suki fell in behind him. "After all, I'm a dragon."

TO THE BUS!

All things considered, Suki was taking things rather well.

Once they had established that Danny was a real dragon—not a bearded water dragon, not a Komodo dragon, but a real honest-to-goodness mythological dragon—she seemed to relax.

"You're very calm," said Wendell.

"I'm convinced he's delusional," said Suki.

"No, he really isn't. I've seen him breathe fire. Well, once."

"It's harder than it looks," said Danny.

"Ah."

Danny's house was pleasant, airy, and smelled faintly of brimstone. Danny's mother was upstairs working, but came down when she heard the front door slam.

Wendell introduced Suki, while Danny raided the fridge.

"Mom," he said, when everybody had been mutually introduced, and Mrs. Dragonbreath was getting out cookies, "who do we know that might know about Japanese mythology?"

"Your great-grandfather," said Mrs. Dragonbreath promptly. "He lives just outside of Izumo Province in Japan." She tapped a claw thoughtfully against the cookie jar.

I HAVEN'T SEEN GRANDDAD IN AGES...

"Right!" Danny stuffed a few extra cookies in his backpack. "We'll be back, Mom. Got to go track down some ninjas."

"Have fun, dear." Mrs. Dragonbreath headed for the stairs. "I have to finish this article tonight, so we'll have to have leftover pizza for dinner."

"Excellent . . ." Danny tapped his claws together. Real live ninjas, a trip to mythological Japan, and pizza for dinner two nights running. Could life get any better?

Wendell slowly lifted a finger
and Danny looked up.

"We'd better head to the bus," said Danny grimly. "It doesn't look like we've got much time."

"So let me get this straight . . ." said Suki, who was obviously holding on to calm by the tips of her fingers. "We're going to take the bus."

"Yup."

"To mythological Japan."

"Yup."

"To see your great-grandfather."

THAT'S THE PLAN. WE MISSED THE THREE 'O CLOCK, BUT WE CAN STILL MAKE THE THREE FIFTEEN...

"Just go with it," Wendell advised. "We took a bus to the Sargasso Sea last month, and that's in the middle of the Atlantic Ocean."

"But this isn't *possible*," said Suki. "I had to take a plane. It took forever."

The city bus pulled up with a hiss of brakes, and all three climbed on.

Suki stared at Wendell for a moment, then folded her arms and settled grimly back into her seat. Wendell winced.

They rode the bus in silence for nearly twenty minutes, past the mall and the library and the dollar theater. Several passengers got off. The only people left on the bus were the driver and an old woman who was snoring gently among her bags of groceries.

The bus pulled out of the theater parking lot, swung to the right, and entered a patch of trees. After a minute, the trees thinned out and seemed to lose their branches. A dusting of white covered the ground.

"Here we are," said Danny. Suki was staring in openmouthed astonishment.

"That's . . . that's *bamboo!* And snow?! And—was that a *shrine*?!"

"Told you," said Danny, without any particular heat. Wendell hadn't believed him the first time either. He pulled the cord, and the bus rumbled to a halt. The driver let them out.

"This isn't really Japan, is it?" Suki asked the driver. "I mean, it's like . . . Japantown or . . . something . . . right?"

The driver rolled her eyes. Since she was a chameleon, there was a lot of eye to roll. "What does it say on the schedule?"

"Mythical Japan," said Danny helpfully.

"Then that's what it is. If you have a problem, please take it up with the transit authority. They have a 1-800 number. Now, if you don't mind, I have a schedule to keep . . ." The chameleon looked pointedly toward the bus stop. Wendell grabbed Suki's arm and steered her off the bus.

"This is not possible . . ." said Suki plaintively, staring up at the bamboo. "I mean . . . the *plane* . . . I had a six-hour layover in Detroit . . ."

"Dragons aren't possible either," said Danny cheerfully. "But we manage. Now, let's see . . ." He lifted his snout and sniffed the air. "Granddad's place should be . . . thataway." He started off into the bamboo forest.

"Do you know that with some kind of special dragon sense?" asked Suki, hurrying to keep up.

"Nah." Danny tapped his nose. "Granddad always rubs this awful camphor stuff on his joints. He says they ache. You can smell it for miles."

Now that Danny mentioned it, Wendell did detect a distinct smell coming from the northeast—camphor and mint and the faint, familiar scent of brimstone. He squared his shoulders and set off into the woods after Danny.

NINJA QUEEN

The bamboo forest was surprisingly dense for not having much in the way of branches, but they rapidly found a path in the direction of the smell. The snow was less than an inch deep, and in patches, the dark earth of the forest floor showed through. It was cold, but not painfully so.

"You doing okay?" Wendell asked Suki in an undertone as they plodded along the path.

"Yeah . . ." Suki shrugged. "I mean . . . it's awfully strange, but I've had ninjas chasing me for three days, so I should be used to strange things by now."

Danny grinned to himself. Suki was pretty tough. You know, for a girl.

After they'd walked for half an hour, the bamboo thinned out and the path led into a cobblestone walkway. At the end of the walkway was a small neat house with a pagoda-style roof and an entryway guarded by stone dogs.

The smell of camphor was eye-wateringly strong now. Wendell and Suki inched past the stone dogs and looked around nervously.

Danny, being Danny, walked up to the front door and pounded on it.

"Eh?" came a querulous voice from inside. "What? Somebody there?"

"It's me, Great-Granddad!" yelled Danny at the top of his lungs.

"What? Danny?"

The door slid open.

Danny's great-grandfather was a dragon, but a different sort of dragon than Wendell had ever seen before. He had a long snaky body, cracked yellow claws, enormous catfish whiskers, and glasses even thicker than Wendell's.

He was also extremely hard of hearing.

"SPEAK UP!" he roared at Wendell after the iguana tried to introduce himself for the third time. "Don't mumble! Kids today, always mumbling! In my day, we knew how to enunciate!" He poked a yellowed claw at Wendell's chest.

"I'm Wen–dell!" Wendell yelled.

"Wanda? You don't look much like a Wanda . . . Are you Martha's girl?"

Wendell turned bright green. Danny snickered.

"I HEARD THAT!"

"Sorry, Great-Granddad . . ."

"Hmmph!" Great-Grandfather Dragonbreath adjusted his glasses. "And who's this?" he asked, leveling his ancient claw at Suki.

The little salamander bowed deeply to the old dragon and said, *Ohayo gozaimasu.*

The effect was immediate. Danny's great-grandfather straightened up and returned the bow, obviously charmed.

"Now that's more like it. Good to know that

some young people still know how to be respectful . . ." He beamed at Suki, then turned his gaze back to Danny. "So what are you doing here, Danny? It's not Thanksgiving already, is it? I told your mother I wasn't coming until that ignoramus she married learns how to cook a turkey without turning it into charcoal—"

"No, Great-Granddad, it's only May and you're thinking of Aunt Kathy's husband," said Danny patiently. "We need to ask your advice."

"Don't marry a man who can't cook a turkey, that's my advice," said Great-Grandfather Dragonbreath, and elbowed Wendell. "Eh, Wanda?"

EH . . . HEH . . . HEH?

They followed him into the surprisingly modern living room. Great-Grandfather Dragonbreath dropped into his recliner with a chinking noise.

When Suki had finished telling her entire story, Danny fished the shuriken out of his pocket and handed it over. "They left this."

The old dragon peered down at it, brow furrowing. "That's the sigil for Spurtongue Clan . . . hmm."

"Do you—" Danny started to ask, and was waved into silence.

Finally, Great-Grandfather Dragonbreath turned to Suki. "Child, I will need to look into your past lives. Will you permit me?"

Suki rubbed the back of her neck. "Will it hurt?"

"It is quite painless." He beckoned her forward with a claw, then laid both hands on top of her head.

Wendell was never able to say afterward what happened in the room, except that it suddenly seemed a great deal smaller and darker, and the ancient dragon seemed a great deal larger and more powerful.

The smell of camphor was replaced with a cold, metallic smell, like snow and steel.

"Yesssssssssss. . . ." The ancient dragon let his breath out in a long hiss. Shadows danced in the corners and over the mantelpiece.

And then it was over. Great-Grandfather Dragonbreath released Suki's head and rubbed his palms together as if they stung. Suki blinked.

"Is that—was that it, sir?"

"Indeed, child." The old dragon pushed himself out from his chair and went into the kitchen. "Tea . . . I need tea . . ."

"What did you find out?" Danny wanted to know.

"Hmmm? Oh." Great-Grandfather Dragonbreath leaned out of the kitchen. "Your little friend is the reincarnation of the great warrior Leaping Sword, who used to rule the Spurtongue Clan of ninja frogs a few hundred years ago."

Suki's jaw dropped.

"Ooh! Ooh! Do me next!" Danny bounced on

his feet. "What I am the reincarnation of?"

"SOMEBODY WHO MUMBLED A LOT!" roared Great-Grandfather Dragonbreath from the kitchen.

"Awwww. . . ."

When he emerged from the kitchen, the old dragon was carrying a tray of tea. He handed a cup to Suki. "Here. Tea makes everything better."

She took the teacup. "What does it mean, sir, that I'm the reincarnation of this warrior?"

"Anyway, it doesn't mean anything. It just is. Danny has an overactive imagination, Wanda and I wear glasses, and you're the reincarnation of an ancient ninja lord." Great-Grandfather Dragonbreath tossed back his tea. "We all have our little quirks."

"That. Is. So. *Cool,*" said Danny, deeply envious.

"So why are the ninjas coming after her?" asked Wendell, trying to ignore the whole Wanda thing. "Are they enemies of the Spurtongue Clan? Are they trying to take revenge on Leaping Sword?"

One of Suki's hands crept out and, apparently quite by accident, grabbed Wendell's arm. Wendell looked down, looked at Suki, and then tried to pretend he hadn't seen anything.

"Oh, heavens, no." Great-Grandfather Dragonbreath waved a hand. "That's the furthest thing from their mind. Spurtongue's after her because they want her to come back and rule them again."

"You mean they want her to be their *queen*?" asked Danny, highly delighted. "Just think of it, Suki! You can wear tabi boots and have shuriken and climb around on rooftops and throw black lotus pollen on your enemies—"

"I don't want to be a ninja!" yelled Suki, yanking her hand off Wendell's arm so that she could grab her head. (Wendell tried not to look disappointed.) "I *want* to be a veterinarian!"

THAT IS SO LIKE A GIRL!

"Gaaaah! Tell her, Great-Granddad! Tell her she wants to be a ninja!"

The old dragon's eyes twinkled. "Very useful profession, veterinarian. I approve of that. Never liked ninjas . . . all that ninjing about."

Danny flailed, and appealed to his last hope. "Wendell, *you* tell her!"

Wendell shook his head slowly. "I dunno, Danny. Ninjas are cool and all . . ."

"Yes! Exactly!"

". . . but they probably won't let you see your family, and I bet they don't spend much time reading comic books. Plus if you screw up a mission, they *kill* you and stuff . . ."

Danny groaned.

"So I think it's cool that there *are* ninjas, but it's probably not much fun *being* a ninja." Wendell pushed his glasses up, looking very serious.

"Thanks, Wendell," said Suki quietly.

Danny heaved a full body sigh, and waved off the resulting smoke. "Fine. . . . Fine."

"So." Danny turned back to his great-grandfather. "If she doesn't want to be a ninja"—he rolled his eyes at this inexplicable behavior—"can we call the Spurtongue Clan and tell them she isn't interested?"

"Ha!" Great-Grandfather Dragonbreath poked a claw at Danny's chest. "You think it's that simple, do you? Ninjas don't give up that easy, boy!"

"Really?" Danny clasped his hands together. "Do we have to defeat the ninjas? Do we have to go into their lair, like the end of *Vengeance of the Thirteen Masters*?"

The old dragon narrowed his eyes. "Can you breathe fire yet, boy?"

... NOT ... EXACTLY ...

"Then you won't last five minutes. Those frogs can do things with a shuriken that would curl your toes." He reached down to the side of his recliner and pulled a lever. The footrest came out and he leaned back. "Ahhh. . . ."

"So what do we do?" asked Suki.

"It's simple." Great-Grandfather Dragonbreath folded his hands and closed his eyes. "You must enlist the aid of the sworn enemies of the Spurtongue Clan—the Geckos of the Golden Chrysanthemum."

"Ooooooh . . ." The name conjured up vivid images in Danny's brain of warrior lizards setting forth to do battle with the amphibian foe. "Where do we find them? Do we have to go on the journey of three mountains, like in *Red Fist of the North,* to find the secret cave and—"

"They're about fifteen minutes down the road. Follow the path, turn left at the mailbox with the golden chrysanthemum on it."

OH.

"I get together with the officers on Tuesdays to play Trivial Pursuit," said his great-grandfather. He sighed. "I'd go with you youngsters, but my joints are old, and I'd just slow you down. Be careful with the geckos. Don't let them talk you into anything foolish." He handed the shuriken back to Danny. "Show them that if they doubt your word."

"Thank you, Dragonbreath-sama," said Suki.

"It was my pleasure, my dear. Nice to meet you, Wanda—"

"Wendell," said Wendell hopelessly.

"—that's what I said. Danny . . ."

Danny hugged the old dragon, who returned it with surprising force. He hung back as his two friends filed into the hallway. "Say, Great-Granddad, can I ask you a question?"

"Yes?" The old dragon peered over his glasses.

"I can't seem to get my fire-breathing right. I did it once, but only because I was really scared. Is there maybe some secret kung fu technique you could teach me?"

WHAT, LIKE "BUDDHA'S BURNING HALITOSIS" OR SOMETHING?

"Yeah!"

Danny's great-grandfather sighed. "First of all, kung fu is Chinese, not Japanese. I realize that those movies you watch are not terribly clear on the difference, but you'd do well not to confuse the two. Secondly . . . well, let's see you try to breathe fire."

"Okay . . ." Danny took a deep breath and tried to summon up the feelings from the last time he'd breathed fire. Unfortunately that had involved a very angry giant squid, and it was hard to get quite the same intensity standing in his great-grandfather's living room.

"Close your eyes," Great-Grandfather Dragonbreath said. "Breathe deeply. Center your chi."

101

HRROOOAGH!

The resulting belch filled the room with smoke. "Cool!" said Danny, pleased. "I don't usually get that much smoke!"

"Yes . . . well . . ." Great-Grandfather Dragonbreath waved the smoke away from his face. "That's something, anyway." He tugged at his whiskers.

"Oh well . . ."
Danny sighed. He'd
been hoping the ancient dragon
would have the magic answer. "Thanks, Great-
Granddad." Danny headed for the door. "I'll
remember what you said."

"Open a window on your way out!" came the
voice behind him. "And quit mumbling!"

NICE BIRDIE

"I wonder what the Geckos of the Golden Chrysanthemum will be like," said Suki as they trudged down the cobblestone road. The snow had drifted over the edges of the paving bricks.

"If they play Trivial Pursuit with my great-granddad, they're probably old," said Danny gloomily. He was feeling rather disillusioned by the whole adventure. Ninjas were apparently jerks, and Suki didn't want to be a ninja queen. Plus, there was no super-secret kung fu technique for breathing fire, and the grand quest to find the enemies of the Spurtongue Clan involved a fifteen-minute walk and a mailbox. If they made a kung fu movie out of this adventure, it would probably be called *Savage Fist of Boredom.*

Worse yet, he thought, watching Wendell and Suki walk at a carefully measured distance from each other—not close enough to be walking together, but not far enough to *not* be walking together—there would be a lengthy romantic subplot.

Those never went well in kung fu movies. Somebody always died tragically. He'd hate for it to be Wendell, and while Suki's insistence that vets were better than ninjas was enough to drive anybody crazy, he didn't want her to die, tragically or otherwise.

Besides, he'd get blamed if anything went wrong. Wendell's mother always blamed Danny when they wound up in the emergency room, which was totally unfair. It was hardly ever his fault. Usually it was just bad luck.

At least fifty percent of the time, anyway.

Danny and Suki looked at him. Wendell shrugged and hunched his shoulders. "What? Mom has some in the garden."

Danny exchanged a glance with Suki. It felt weird, and yet he couldn't shake the feeling that she understood exactly what he was thinking.

They followed the path up to a small ornamental bridge, with nothing much going under it.

"Is there even water in that stream or just rocks?" asked Danny.

"Well, there's something over there—" said Wendell, pointing. "It's something white. It was moving a second ago—there!"

Danny put a hand on the bridge railing and vaulted over it. "I think it's alive!"

The other two hurried off the bridge and into the rock "stream." The rocks were black and slick.

"What *is* it?" asked Wendell, baffled, as they got closer.

"It's a crane!" said Suki.

"A crane?" Danny frowned. He knew what cranes looked like—big, bulky machinery with arms that went dozens of feet into the air. "But it doesn't look anything like—"

"She means the bird, idiot," muttered Wendell, elbowing him.

"I knew that," Danny said.

However graceful the bird might be in flight, once on the ground, the crane was an awkward

flopping scarecrow, all pointy beak and shedding feathers. It flailed its wings, scattering down like falling snow.

"I don't know if it's hurt," said Danny, after a minute. "I think it's stuck. There's something wrapped around its wing."

"Oh, the poor thing," said Suki. "We have to help it!"

The crane hissed at them and struck out with a beak like a javelin. Danny hadn't known that cranes could hiss, or that they were quite so good at it.

"Um," said Wendell.

"I'm all for helping," said Danny, "but that thing doesn't seem to want much help."

"It's a bird. Birds calm down if you cover their heads," said Suki matter-of-factly. She stuck out a hand. "One of you, give me your shirt."

Danny and Wendell looked at Suki. They looked at the crane. They looked at each other.

"Um," said Wendell again.

Suki glared at them both. The crane hissed. Wendell sighed and stripped off his shirt.

"There's a good birdie," said Suki in a singsong, approaching the crane with the striped shirt in her hands. Wendell stood shivering in his scales. Danny snickered.

"Good birdie . . . nice birdie . . ." Suki moved closer. The crane watched her with hard, bright eyes. The beak scissored open and another hiss drifted out.

She tossed the shirt. It landed over the bird's eyes. She stepped in fearlessly and grabbed the other end of the shirt, knotting it loosely over the bird's head. Danny and Wendell held their breath, expecting her to become a salamander-kebab, but the crane stayed silent.

"There," said Suki with satisfaction, turning to the injured wing. "Danny, hold its head. Wendell, help me stretch out its wing."

"Um," said Wendell a third time.

Danny had done a lot of things in his life that,

upon careful reflection in the ambulance, had been needlessly risky.

It did not take much careful reflection to realize that holding the head of a gigantic, angry, hissing bird was maybe not the best idea.

He did it anyway. If Suki—a girl—was able to tie a blindfold around the crane, refusing to hold its head would be pure cowardice. Wendell would never let him hear the end of it, and Wendell was terrified of all kinds of perfectly safe things, like gunpowder and bottle rockets.

"Here. You stretch the wing out—gently!—

and I'll get this thing off . . . looks like some kind of strap . . ."

Danny waited for the crane to get tired of Suki manhandling its wing. He wondered if he'd even feel the snap, or if he'd just suddenly be short an arm. Or a head. Maybe he'd just have a beak stabbed all the way through him. That would probably be best. They could still have an open-casket funeral, which they generally didn't do if you were missing a head.

"Oh, you poor thing," murmured Suki. "Your poor wing! Who did this to you?"

The crane, being a crane, said nothing, but did try to pull its wing back.

"Hold it steady!" Suki snapped at Wendell, in a much less soothing tone than she used on the bird. Wendell sighed and braced his feet, trying to stretch out the bird's wing.

Astonishingly, the crane still hadn't killed him. Maybe Suki had been right about covering their eyes.

"There," said the salamander, sounding satisfied. She stepped back, holding some sort of black leather strip with weights on the end. "All done. It's lost a couple of feathers, but it didn't break the skin. Wendell, let it go."

Wendell did not need to be told twice. He jumped back to a safe distance. Suki waved Danny away from the crane's head, then carefully pulled the blindfold free and stepped back out of range herself.

"There you go," she said. "All better."

The crane shook itself, then got its legs under it in a complicated motion that reminded Danny of someone jacking up a car with a flat tire. Standing, the crane was at least twice as tall as any of them. It made Big Eddy look small.

The crane stretched out its injured wing carefully, flexed it once or twice, then folded it back against its side.

Bright gold eyes regarded Suki. The crane turned its head from side to side, peering at her carefully. It was impossible to read anything in that flat, emotionless gaze.

It took a step toward Suki.

Next to Danny, Wendell tensed. Danny wondered if there was any chance he could breathe fire if things got messy—sure, he really couldn't do it on command, but he *had* done it that one time when the squid was about to eat Wendell, and maybe if the crane was about to eat Suki he could figure something out—

It took another step forward. Suki stood her ground, but Danny heard her gulp.

Center your chi, Danny's grandfather had said. Let the energy of fire fill your lungs. Was that the energy of fire or indigestion? Oh well, only one way to find out. . . . He took a deep breath.

Then—and Danny could scarcely believe it—the crane *bowed* to Suki, like an actor in a movie.

Suki bowed back.

The crane straightened up, turned, and took three running strides along the black rock streambed. Then it launched into the air, seeming to barely miss the green bamboo trunks. In a moment it vanished against the white of the clouded sky.

Danny realized that he was still holding his breath, and let out a cloud of smoke. Wendell coughed and fanned at his face.

Suki handed Wendell back his shirt and looked desperately smug. Still, Danny thought, he had to admit, she'd probably earned it.

"Vet, huh?" he said.

"You'd better believe it."

HELLO, GECKO

The thing on the crane's wing turned out to be a bola, which Danny recognized from *Nine Nights of Ninjas*. A bola was a long leather strap with two heavy spiked weights on the ends. Both weights had the spiral sigil of the Spurtongue Clan.

"I really don't like those guys," said Suki. "I mean, reincarnated ninja lords, fine. But attacking innocent birds is just cruel."

"If you agreed to be their queen, you could open a ninja animal hospital," said Danny hopefully.

Suki actually appeared to think about this.

Whatever thoughts she was having, however, stopped at the sight of the gate.

The gate was at least twenty feet tall and had big iron hinges and giant door knockers like steel chrysanthemums. There were inset panels on the frame, showing stylized geckos.

Danny would have preferred something with rusted metal spikes, possibly dripping blood, and the bones of the geckos' enemies lined up on top, but he had to admit that was more a matter of personal preference.

Neither Wendell nor Suki moved.

"Are we sure this is a good idea?" Wendell asked. "If they're the oldest enemies of the Spur-tongue, and you're the reincarnation of the great Spurtongue leader, it doesn't seem like they'd be very happy to see you."

Suki chewed on her lower lip. "I don't know . . ."

"You worry too much, Wendell," said Danny, and reached for the chrysanthemum ring.

Wendell rolled his eyes.

The booming of metal on wood had only just faded when they heard footsteps, and the door creaked open.

I'M NOT THE MAILMAN. I THINK YOU PLAY TRIVIAL PURSUIT WITH MY GREAT-GRANDFATHER, THOUGH.
OLD RYUU DRAGONBREATH? HE CHEATS.

There didn't seem to be anything Danny could say to this. Fortunately the gecko warrior opened the door, saying, "Well, cheater or not, any friend of Dragonbreath . . ." He gestured them inside.

They filed through the door, and froze in their tracks.

"Finally . . ." breathed Danny.

The home of the Geckos of the Golden Chrysanthemum had no metal spikes, no piles of bones, and in fact, there were several cherry trees planted around the compound, blossoming despite the season.

But the geckos themselves made up for it. There were a half dozen strolling around the courtyard, all of them in elegant armor, carrying tall halberds* or lacquer-sheathed swords. Even Danny, who had seen every martial arts movie ever badly dubbed into English, was impressed. Maybe they wouldn't have to name this *Savage Fist of Boredom* after all.

"So what brings you here?" asked the gate-keeper. "If it's about your great-granddad's lawn mower, tell him he's not getting it back until I get my hedge trimmer—"

*COOL ~~NINJA~~ SAMURAI FACT #3:
A HALBERD IS A TRADITIONAL SAMURAI WEAPON, CONSISTING OF AN AXEBLADE ON THE END OF A LONG POLE.

"We need you to make the Spurtongue Clan leave Suki alone!" Wendell blurted.

It wasn't as if all the armor clacked simultaneously or anything. Not exactly. It was just that Danny became exquisitely aware, without even looking, that they had everybody's full attention.

He looked anyway. Sure enough, all of the geckos were watching. One or two had even drawn their swords.

"I think," said the gatekeeper, sounding more like a samurai and less like somebody worried about a hedge trimmer, "you need to talk to the lord."

The leader of the Geckos of the Golden Chrysanthemum was actually a little shorter than the gatekeeper and quite broad for a gecko. His black lacquered armor was very bright, but not as bright as his eyes.

"Lord Takeshi," said the gatekeeper, putting a fist over his heart, "I have brought you the great-grandson of Ryuu Dragonbreath and his companions."

Lord Takeshi nodded to Danny. "Your great-grandfather is a good friend to us. Although he cheats at—"

"Trivial Pursuit," Danny said wearily, "yes, I've heard."

"Well, enough of such concerns. What brings you here, scion of Dragonbreath, with the name of Spurtongue on your lips?"

Danny brightened. Now *this* was more like it!

WELL, IT STARTED WITH THESE NINJAS COMING AFTER WENDELL'S GIRLFRIEND SUKI . . .
SHE IS NOT MY GIRLFRIEND!

The story didn't take long to tell. Suki told most of it, although Danny had to explain about the bus and the Spurtongue shuriken, and Wendell kept interrupting with inconvenient facts and arguing that Suki wasn't his girlfriend.

Lord Takeshi mostly listened in silence. But when Danny got to the bit about his great-grandfather discovering Suki's past life, Takeshi held out a hand. "Come forward, daughter."

Suki's gills fluttered nervously, but she lifted her chin and approached the kneeling gecko.

Lord Takeshi put his hands on her shoulders and peered into her eyes, the way the eye doctor peered into Wendell's when deciding if the iguana needed new glasses. "Leaping Sword," he said. "I can see her at the bottom of your mind . . ."

Suki gulped.

"Don't worry, daughter." The old warrior patted her shoulder kindly. "The Geckos of the Golden Chrysanthemum have not fallen so far that we would take vengeance on a child."

"She's not going to try to take over my brain or something, is she?" asked Suki nervously.

Takeshi shook his head. "She is you, and you cannot take over your own mind."

"So what do we do about Spurtongue?" asked Wendell. "Can you help us?"

Lord Takeshi rubbed his chin. "Perhaps. Unfortunately it is not so simple as one might wish. I and my warriors have the might to battle Spurtongue, and we would be glad to do so . . . but we do not know how to find them."

"Essentially correct," said Takeshi. "But you might be able to help us."

"You want us to find the ninjas?" Danny frowned. He might be almost just about a kung fu master—really close, anyway—but tracking ninjas seemed like a different sort of job. If a whole fortress full of samurai geckos couldn't do it . . .

"Not precisely." Takeshi grinned. "I want the ninjas to find *you*."

NINJA BAIT

"This is a stupid plan," said Wendell as they tromped through the bamboo forest. "I mean, this is really a bad idea. I don't think we should have agreed to this."

"I don't think we had any choice," said Suki. "Well, I didn't have any choice. You shouldn't have come, though. If anything happens to you because of me—"

"Oh, for cryin' out loud," said Danny, hoping to head off any mushy stuff, "will you two love-birds give it a rest?"

Wendell and Suki both glared at him, then sighed simultaneously. As horrible as the notion of losing his best friend to love's saccharine clutches was, Danny was starting to think they were made for each other. How revolting.

"He's right," said Suki.

"I know," said Wendell.

Danny thought he might throw up.

Best friend or not, Wendell was starting to annoy him. When Lord Takeshi had explained his plan to let the ninja frogs capture Suki and thus lead the geckos back to their ninja lair, Wendell had immediately claimed it was too dangerous for her to go alone. And when Danny had pointed out—completely logically!—that since it was Suki the frogs *wanted,* she was the only one who *was* safe, the iguana had given him such a look!

It's not like Danny had been suggesting they let her go off and be bait by herself. Danny wouldn't have missed the chance to see a real ninja fortress for the world.

"A net trap! That is so classic! It's just like the one in *Shao-lin Renegades*! This is awesome!"

"If you're quite done," said Wendell acidly, trying to get Danny's foot out of his face, "maybe you can tell us how to get *out*?"

"Oh." Danny chewed on his lower lip. "That might be a problem. I don't think I know the Freezing Wolf Fist move, so I can't freeze the ropes and shatter them, like in the movie . . ."

Wendell tried to put his head in his hands, but his hands were pinned between the rope and Suki's tail. He groaned instead.

"Well," said Suki philosophically, "at least we know the ninjas are somewhere around here."

Danny considered. He could try breathing fire, but he was wedged at such an awkward angle, he'd probably fry both his friends and his own knee. On the other hand, he still had that shuriken. He began trying to work his fingers toward his shirt pocket.

"This was a horribly bad idea," moaned Wendell.

"If you'd just move your knee out of my back—"

There were four ninja frogs. They stared at the trio with large, goggling eyes, and then finally one spoke.

"The oyabun will be pleased to see you."

"What's an oyabun?" whispered Danny.

"The head of an underworld clan," whispered Suki. "The one in charge."

One of the frogs leaped up onto the net—Wendell recoiled from a face-full of slimy toes—and cut the rope. He leaped clear. The trio of kids crashed to the ground with a thud.

SNOW IS NOT NEARLY AS SOFT AS IT LOOKS.

The frogs surrounded them. Strong, slick fingers grabbed Danny's arms and hauled him backward. The one who had spoken before nodded to Danny's captor and said, "Tie their hands."

Another frog grabbed Wendell and produced a rope.

It occurred to Danny that while it was all very well to talk about being bait and being deliberately captured and so forth, once it was *actually happening* to you, it was a bit alarming.

As the frog pulled Danny's hands behind him and began tying them, Danny realized that if the geckos didn't show up, they might be in very serious trouble.

Still, maybe he wasn't entirely without resources . . .

"My great-granddad is Ryuu Dragonbreath, so you'd better be careful!" Danny said, trying not to sound as nervous as he felt.

The leader paused, his gaze sharpening. "Ryuu Dragonbreath?"

Danny nodded. *Let this work,* he thought, *and I will send Great-Granddad a handwritten thank-you note like Mom's always nagging me to do—*

"Tie that one extra tight," the ninja leader ordered. "His great-grandfather cheats at Trivial Pursuit."

Great.

THE FROG-FATHER

Danny was bitterly disappointed.

He'd gone to all this trouble. He'd been captured and tied up and marched through the woods, during which he'd had to listen to Wendell ask Suki if she was okay approximately once a minute. (Even Suki had apparently gotten tired of this, finally answering: "I'm STILL FINE, Wendell." It had gotten them a snicker from the ninja frogs.)

And this would all have been fine—it was an adventure, after all, and these things happened—if he could have finally seen the ninja fortress of Spurtongue Clan.

But no. The ninjas had blindfolded all three of them. There were probably weapons and pointy things and ninjas doing fabulous secret ninja stuff all around them, and all Danny could see was the inside of a piece of cloth.

The only reason he even knew they were in the fortress was because the ground underfoot had stopped being snow and had started being rock, and then gravel for a little bit, and now was some kind of slick, cold tile.

The hand on his back stopped pushing him forward. A moment later, the blindfold was removed, and Danny, Wendell, and Suki stood in a row, blinking in the light.

They were in a hall that looked a little bit like a church without any pews. There was nothing to indicate that it was the home of a diabolical secret ninja clan. Danny sighed.

Before them, behind a moat of dozens of flickering candles, sat the oyabun.

Presumably the oyabun must have been a ninja himself at some point, but it was hard to believe. He was gigantic, bulging out in every direction, his eyes as large as Danny's head. If he had tried to leap lightly along a rooftop, he would have taken out several stories.

"Well, well, well . . . Leaping Sword's current incarnation. *So* considerate of you to save us the trouble of finding you," purred the massive frog, steepling his webbed fingers in front of him.

"If this was my ninja fortress, I would totally put up some posters," muttered Danny under his breath.

"I came to ask you to leave me alone!" said Suki, stepping forward. She looked very small in front of the giant amphibian.

"We aren't going to do that," said the oyabun. "We need you to be our next leader, after I retire."

"Nothing fancy," Danny said, to no one in particular. "The movie poster for *Nine Nights of Ninjas,* maybe. Recruitment posters. Something."

"I'm very flattered," said Suki, obviously trying to be polite. "But I don't think I'd be a very good leader. There's been some kind of mistake."

"No mistake," said the oyabun. His voice was thick and bubbly, like warm mud. "You're going to stay here, and you're going to be a ninja. This is really not open for debate."

"I don't want to be a ninja," said Suki, clenching her hands into fists. "I *want* to be a veterinarian!"

YES, YES. MY PREDECESSOR WANTED TO BE A FIREFIGHTER. WE DON'T ALWAYS GET WHAT WE WANT.

"Please, Mr. Oyabun," squeaked Wendell, bowing awkwardly. "Suki knows what she wants to be, and it's not a ninja. You said that your predecessor wanted to be a firefighter. Isn't there something you wanted to be as a child? A dream you still wish you could have followed?"

Danny turned and stared at Wendell. He hadn't

known the iguana had a speech like that in him, even if it was kind of corny.

For a second, it looked like it might work. Wendell was practically trembling with earnestness, and the ninja frogs fidgeted and wiped at their eyes.

It occurred to Danny that one did not become the leader of a diabolical ninja clan by giving in to sentimental speeches.

"Well, I tried," muttered Wendell, deflating and hunching his shoulders.

"Good speech, though." Danny punched his best friend appreciatively in the shoulder. "Maybe you can try it out the next time Mom grounds me."

"If you are quite through," said the oyabun, sounding bored, "we can see about assigning you your quarters and fitting you for something in black tabi—"

Suki took a deep breath.

"I won't do it!" she yelled, staring defiantly up into the face of the oyabun. Her thick tail lashed. "You might be able to keep me prisoner, but I won't be a ninja! I won't be your leader! You'll have to let me go!"

The giant frog tilted his head to one side and smiled a slow, slimy smile.

HOT LAVA

"What *I* want to know is how the ninjas got a live volcano!" said Wendell.

Danny sighed. Here they were, about to die, and as usual, Wendell was preoccupied with trivialities.

The volcano in question was a perfectly respectable smoking volcano, the sort where primitive islanders throw human sacrifices in order to appease the gods in a certain type of movie. The ninjas had erected a platform on one side, and there was a long walkway out to the middle.

Danny and Wendell were tied together and had been dumped onto the platform like a sack of potatoes. The side of Danny facing the volcano was getting uncomfortably warm.

He had a bad feeling that the walkway was going to figure prominently in their future.

"And there are no hand rails," said Wendell, a slightly hysterical edge to his voice. "That's just not *safe*."

THEY'RE NINJAS, WENDELL. THEY DON'T USE HAND RAILS!

The ninja frog guarding them leaned over. "It came with the fortress, actually. Japan is really very seismically active, and since we bought the whole place from a mad scientist who was looking to retire, it came with its own volcano."

Danny and Wendell stared at him. The ninja smiled in a friendly fashion, notwithstanding the fact that he was holding them prisoner at the edge of a pit of roiling lava.

"Once we cleared out the old lawn furniture, it was a very nice place to relax in winter."

Unable to stop himself, Danny added, "Plus you can throw prisoners into it!"

From where they sat, Danny could hear Suki and the oyabun talking. Suki was being held between two ninjas, and the massive figure of the oyabun loomed over her. The ninjas had decided that Suki should be dressed more appropriately for her station, and had given her a black kimono and an elaborate headdress. Danny was not sure how many ninja frogs it had taken to wrestle her into the thing, but judging by Suki's expression, he was betting on double digits.

"This is really very simple," the giant frog said. "In a few minutes time, we will drop your little friends into the volcano. Now, if you were willing to accept your place as our leader, you could, of course, give an order to prevent that."

Suki looked pale. "What if

I agreed to be your leader, and then ordered you to let me go?"

The oyabun sighed. "Then you would no longer be our leader, and we would recapture you immediately. You would all wind up back in the volcano, everyone would be put to a great deal of trouble and annoyance, and I would be very put out."

"D-don't do it, Suki!" yelled Wendell, determined to be brave despite trembling uncontrollably.

"Being a ninja might be really cool, Suki!" yelled Danny.

DANNY!

WHAT?
IT MIGHT BE.

"I don't know what you're worried about," said Danny. "The geckos should arrive any minute."

"Then where are they?" Wendell hissed.

This was an excellent question. If the geckos were going to come charging to the rescue, they were certainly taking their time about it.

"I'm sure they'll be here," said Danny. "Relax. Suki's buying us time."

"Push them over the pit," ordered the oyabun.

"No!" squeaked the salamander, then promptly kicked the oyabun in the ankle. The oyabun rolled his eyes and waved a hand, and one of the ninja frogs said, "Excuse me, scion of Leaping Sword," and pulled her hands behind her.

Danny didn't see what happened to Suki next. He was a bit preoccupied with the ninja frogs hooking the ropes to a pulley and swinging them out over the pit. A blast of hot air roared off the volcano, like standing in front of an oven, only a lot worse.

It occurred to Danny that possibly it was time to start helping themselves.

DON'T WORRY! I THINK I CAN BREATHE FIRE!
WE'RE DANGLING OVER HOT LAVA! MORE FIRE IS NOT HELPFUL HERE!

The ropes fell away. Unfortunately, since those ropes had been holding Danny and Wendell together, they had only a split second to grab for handholds. Wendell shrieked.

SWOOOOOOP!

Danny felt Wendell slip, felt his own grip fail—and then, before he could even panic, he was rising up on—a cloud?

It was the giant crane.

Wendell was sprawled across the great bird's back like a lizard in a featherbed. Danny felt himself start to slide on the slick feathers and grabbed for the bird's neck as it banked into a turn. Hot air rising from the mouth of the volcano caught the bird's feathers and lifted it high into the sky, until Suki and the ninja frogs and the shocked figure of the oyabun were tiny specks on the edge of the volcano.

"GET THEM!" roared the oyabun as the crane wheeled overhead. "Stop them! Shoot that bird down!"

"We have to go back!" Wendell yelled, crawling forward across the feathers. "We can't leave Suki!"

Whether it understood English or not, the crane seemed to agree, because it pulled its wings in and spiraled downward toward the volcano.

"Shoot them!" the oyabun yelled again, but nobody seemed to be shooting. In fact, except for the oyabun, nobody was paying attention to such trivial matters as a gigantic, potentially frog-eating bird swooping down from the sky.

"Master!" cried one of the ninja frogs as the crane swept low. "Master, the geckos are attacking!"

WHAT?!

"Suki!" yelled Wendell. "Suki, JUMP!"

Whatever else one might say about Suki, girl or not, ninja or not, Danny had to admit one thing.

She had guts.

The salamander wrenched loose of her distracted captor, dove under the belly of the oyabun—and threw herself into the volcano.

The crane dove too. Wendell shrieked again, and Danny let out a noise that he would later claim was a whoop of victory. The whole world skewed sideways, the crane practically stood on its head in the air, and Danny and Wendell stared directly into the lava.

Suki smacked down hard on the crane's back, nearly flattening Wendell. Danny grabbed for the back of her dress, Wendell got part of her tail, and the three of them somehow clung to the back of the crane's back as it soared up from the volcano.

"Did the geckos really come?" Suki panted.

Wendell pointed downward as the crane leveled out and began flying, with broad wingbeats, back across the forest.

"Look for yourself," he said.

OUT OF THE BAMBOO

The crane set them down not far from the bus stop. Whether it understood the bus system, or just understood Suki pointing down and saying "There, please!" was open to debate.

With its enormous wings folded up, the crane looked a great deal smaller. It turned its head from side to side, peering down at them, and then it fanned its tail a little and bowed.

Danny and Wendell bowed back. Suki started to bow, then stepped forward and hugged the crane's leg, which was as high as she could reach.

"Thank you, Crane-san. You saved our lives."
Danny rolled his eyes. "That is so like a girl."
"What should she do, give it a handshake?"

They stood in the woods, staring after the crane long after it had vanished. Evening was coming on, and it was getting dark. Nobody said anything as they trudged wearily toward the road.

"Why the long faces? You won, didn't you?"

"Great-Granddad!" Danny ran forward.

His great-grandfather was leaning against the bus stop sign. He slapped Danny on the back. "Hi, Danny, Suki. Wanda, glad you made it . . ."

Wendell sighed.

"I thought I'd bring you out some tea," said the old dragon. "Craneback riding is awfully cold."

"How did you know?" Danny asked.

I'M OLD, NOT DEAD! BESIDES, YOU COULD HEAR *THAT* RUCKUS TEN MILES OFF.

He handed out paper cups full of steaming tea.

"Thank you," said Suki. "Please—do you know if the frogs will leave me alone now?"

"After that beating?" Great-Grandfather Dragonbreath grinned. "It'll take 'em years before they dare stick their snouts out of their fortress. I think you'll be fine." He picked up his walking stick. "And now, since the bus is on its way, I'll be off. Say hello to your mother for me, Danny." He paused, glancing back over his shoulder. "You did good. Even without breathing fire."

Great-Granddad Dragonbreath tromped off through the snow, occasionally whacking bamboo with his walking stick when it didn't get out of his way fast enough (or at all).

The kids drank their hot tea in silence until the bus pulled up. They climbed wearily aboard.

Suki sat down next to the window, and Wendell shyly sat down next to her.

"Um." Suki looked at Wendell.

"Um." Wendell looked at Suki.

"Did you see that?!" Danny draped himself over the back of the seat in front of them. "When all the geckos showed up? Wasn't that the coolest thing *ever*?!"

THE GECKOS WERE ALL LIKE "WE'LL GET YOU, NINJAS!" AND THE NINJAS WERE LIKE "ARRRGH, GECKOS!"

Wendell sighed. "It *was* pretty cool," he agreed.

"But the coolest thing was the crane," said Suki.

"Eh, I don't know." Danny rubbed the back of his neck. "It was awfully drafty up there."

"I think I would have gotten seasick after a while," Wendell agreed.

"No way!" Suki crossed her arms. "The crane was totally the best!"

The argument lasted for the entire bus ride back to the stop by Danny's house. If there was a distinct transition between mythological Japan and the park on the way to the mall, none of them noticed it.

When the bus dropped them off—and suddenly their adventure was well and truly over—they found themselves tongue-tied again.

"Um," said Suki. "I . . . uh . . . guess I'll see you guys tomorrow at school."

"Um," said Wendell.

"Um. Yeah," said Danny.

They all stood around, staring in different directions.

"I should get going," said Suki. "I'm already out late, and my host parents will get worried."

"Yeah."

"Definitely."

Suki started to turn away, then stopped. "Thank

you, guys," she said, and gave both of them a quick hug. Then she turned and began walking away very quickly.

"Yeck," muttered Danny, wiping at his arms. "I suppose now I've got cooties. Eh, Wendell . . . Wendell?"

BACK TO SCHOOL

"So *do* you think the ninjas will bother you again?" asked Wendell as he, Danny, and Suki sat at lunch the next day. Big Eddy wandered by in the distance, like an elephant crossing a linoleum savannah, but the trio was trying to ignore him. Danny hadn't even protested eating lunch with a girl. After all, it wasn't just any girl, it was *Suki*.

Besides, Big Eddy had stolen Danny's lunch on the way out of the cafeteria line, and Suki had donated her potato chips so he didn't go hungry.

"Well . . ." Suki set her sandwich down, glancing

around to see if anyone was watching. "I found a note in my locker this morning." She held it out.

"So that's that, then," said Wendell, leaning back.

"I guess so," said Suki.

Danny laughed into his potato chips.

After a minute, he realized that both Wendell and Suki were staring at him.

"What?"

"What's that supposed to mean?" asked Suki, narrowing her eyes.

"Oh, relax," said Danny, waving a chip. "I'm sure you'll be fine for a while. By the time somebody comes after you because you kebabed their great-great-great-grandmother, you'll probably be old. Like in high school or something."

"Oh." Suki relaxed. "That's okay, then . . ."

SO LONG, FAREWELL

THREE WEEKS LATER . . .

"So I heard today was Suki's last day," said Danny as he and Wendell walked home together.

"Yup," said the iguana. "She's going back home to Japan."

"You gonna be okay?" Danny asked.

"Sure," said Wendell. He shrugged. "She promised that she'd write."

"That's good."

Wendell punched him. Danny nobly accepted this expression of his friend's grief without retaliating.

They walked in silence for a while.